WHAT MAKES
My Daddy Best?

By Burton Albert

Illustrated by Kathryn Mitter

Little Simon

Note to Adults

This book includes two pages of stickers that can be added to
the pictures. Please encourage your child to choose stickers
that relate to each scene and to place them accordingly
wherever possible. For example, there are stickers of seagulls
that can be added to the boardwalk scene.

In memory of my father and of Thomas C. Bent—B.A.

 LITTLE SIMON

An imprint of Simon & Schuster Children's Publishing Division
1230 Avenue of the Americas, New York, New York 10020
Text copyright © 1998 by Burton Albert
Illustrations copyright © 1998 by Kathryn Mitter
All rights reserved including the right of reproduction
in whole or in part in any form.
LITTLE SIMON and colophon are registered
trademarks of Simon & Schuster.
A Stickers 'n' Shapes Book is a
trademark of Simon & Schuster.
Manufactured in Indonesia
10 9 8 7 6 5 4 3 2 1
ISBN 0-689-81230-2

What makes my daddy laugh?
Flippity-flopping
and shrinking in half.
That makes my daddy laugh.

What makes my daddy moan?
Dripping ice cream
from a cone.
That makes my daddy moan.

What makes my daddy sniff?
Splashing myself
with shaving whiff.
That makes my daddy sniff.

What makes my daddy shout?
Cluttering stairs
with toys about.
That makes my daddy shout.

What makes my daddy puff?
Jumping in
with his garden stuff.
That makes my daddy puff.

What makes my daddy snap?
Teasing our pups
as he tries to nap.
That makes my daddy snap.

WORLD'S
BEST
DAD

What makes my daddy scream?
Kicking a goal
for the soccer team.
That makes my daddy scream.

What makes my daddy sigh?
Asking "where" and "why"
about the sky.
That makes my daddy sigh.

What makes my daddy sneeze?
Sprinkling pepper
upon his peas.
That makes my daddy sneeze.

What makes my daddy cheer?
Pedaling a bike—
learning to steer.
That makes my daddy cheer.

What dy hum?

my teum.

makes my daddy hum.

What makes my daddy best?
Feeling his love—
the hug of his chest.
That makes my daddy best!

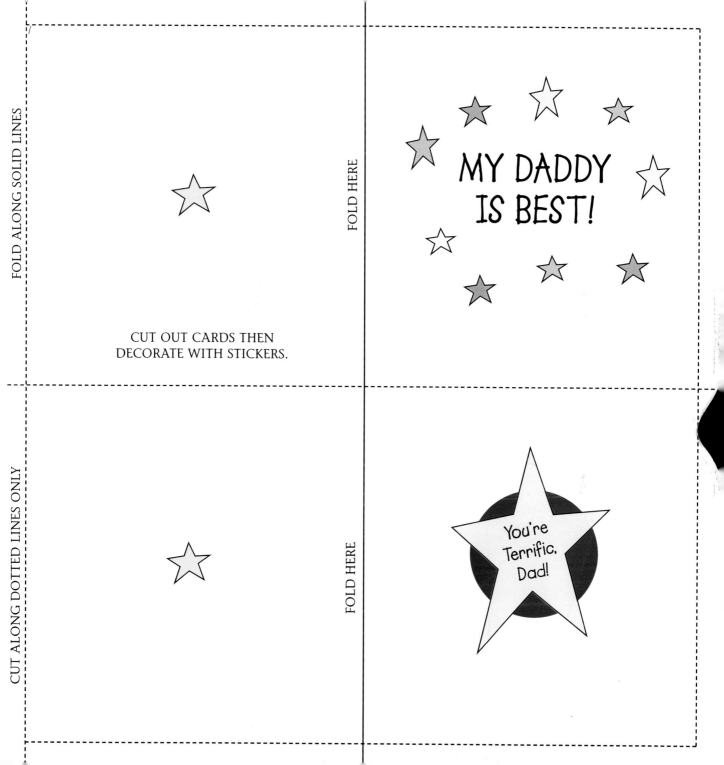

FOLD ALONG SOLID LINES

FOLD HERE

CUT OUT CARDS THEN
DECORATE WITH STICKERS.

MY DADDY
IS BEST!

CUT ALONG DOTTED LINES ONLY

FOLD HERE

You're
Terrific,
Dad!

Love, Eden

Love, *[signature]*